THE CREDO OF COMRADE JANUARY

ROBERT BAGNALL

Published by Water Dragon Publishing
waterdragonpublishing.com

ISBN 978-1-962538-35-0 (Trade Paperback)

FIRST EDITION

10 9 8 7 6 5 4 3 2 1

THE CREDO OF COMRADE JANUARY

"**T**HAT SOMETIMES HAPPENS TOO," the chief prosecutor said.

The justice minister had been driven in a black limousine all the way from Moscow, an additional sixty gallons of gasoline in a slipper tank welded to the roof to ensure sufficient range. It made the car wallow on the icy roads, disturbing him from signing death warrants.

The chief prosecutor, a weaselly man with sunken eyes and cheaply dyed hair, met the vehicle, armed with an umbrella for the minister to shelter under. The sky was clear and bright. The minister rolled his eyes despairingly, recognizing obsequiousness when he saw it.

Trailed by a coterie of guards and assistants, plus the minister's personal secretary pitting pocket-watch against schedule, the two men trotted up marble steps of the municipal palace of government and in through tall mahogany doors. Sentries clicked their heels as the circus passed. Down staircases and along labyrinthine corridors they swept until they came to an anonymous green metal door blocking their way. An oversize key was produced by somebody at the back and passed, hand over hand, to the chief prosecutor at the front, who unlocked the door with a flourish, like a magician producing a rabbit from a hat.

The door opened onto a small snowy courtyard at the bottom of a shaft created where various extensions and additions to the palace of government abutted but failed to adjoin. A select group trooped through. The minister shivered at the all-pervading damp of a space perpetually in shadow, noting the sheer unadorned windowless brick walls — no need for marble or statuary recovered from the Hermitage's ruins here, far away from public view — which towered up five floors on all sides. Snowflakes lazily tumbled from a distant patch of sky. There was no umbrella for him now, he dryly mused.

Two doors accessed the courtyard. One, they — the minister, his secretary, the chief prosecutor, and two guards — had come through. The other, opposite, opened with a groan, and through it came another pair of warders with a barefoot prisoner in thin, grey pajamas. He had the callow look of something starved in darkness, his head shaved, rendered too timid to know where to look. The guards positioned him in the corner where he swayed and shivered, wondering and waiting with hollow bewilderment.

A moment later, another figure stepped through the second door, burly and short, in non-standard khaki coveralls, big leather boots, and a thin black executioner's hood. His movements were dull-witted, bovine. At the sight of the newcomer the prisoner stifled a shriek, cowering fetal into the corner, his eyes like saucers.

"Avakardian," the chief prosecutor whispered to the minister, nodding toward the newcomer, as though clarifying a plot point at the opera. There was pride in his voice.

"Where did you say you found him?"

"In a village. It seems his father had similar talents, although nowhere near as pronounced. His father was born some months after the Pulse. Burnt as a witch, or whatever the male equivalent is. We are trying to acclimatize this one to civilization."

With an animalistic crouch, Avakardian moved in on the prisoner, step by ponderous step, clawed fingers leading. Sunk to his haunches, the prisoner moaned *no, no, no*. Avakardian closed in, the prisoner folding beneath him. The minister shifted for a better view, but the torturer's porcine body had enveloped the stick-like captive who screamed in sudden agony, accompanied by another noise, an audible buzzing, like an unseen wasps' nest, and an odd mixture of smells, both metallic and gastronomic. Searing meat, perhaps.

Avakardian moved away from the whimpering prisoner, now balled up against the junction of brick walls and snow-packed ground. Thin smoke-trails rose from his chest and shoulders, from where Avakardian had gripped him.

"Good God," the minister said, "Just from ... his fingertips?"

"He will need to eat well after this. It saps incredible amounts of energy."

Another smell struck the onlookers, its source plain for all to see.

"That sometimes happens," the chief prosecutor said, and with a flick of his eyes sent two guards trotting back into the building.

The minister curled his lip at the sight of the prisoner's thin sagging pajama bottoms, soiled a steaming mélange of brown and yellow. The guards doused the man with buckets of water, bringing forth new screams of shock.

Avakardian moved in again despite the putrid skink, like a predatory animal delivering the coup de grace, the insect buzzing more pronounced, the screaming louder and more despairing, the smell of burning, charring flesh stronger. The minister could see the captive's bare feet writhing with the current underneath the torturer.

And then Avakardian fell forward into space, a space through which the minister swore he could see — a patch of grass? a patch of grass in sunlight? — jarring a shoulder against the brickwork. He picked himself up, comically confused at his prey's escape.

Dumbfounded, the minister looked to the chief prosecutor for an explanation.

The chief prosecutor chewed his lip as they stepped forward to consider the melted outline in the disturbed snow, a mess of slush and grit where the captive had been, stained brown at one end. He shook his head as Avakardian removed his hood, revealing an uncomprehending face, no more than twenty years old, all puppy fat and piggy eyes.

The prisoner had simply vanished.

"That sometimes happens too," the chief prosecutor repeated.

•   •   •

I was drunk. I was foolish. It was late.

That much I remember.

Someone threatened to perform a polka. Scratchy gramophone music played behind the hubbub of chatter, the fug of tobacco, the clinking of glasses. It felt warm in Sergei Popov's apartment. It felt safe. I felt safe.

"Look at us," I cried. "We are old. All we ever do is talk. When will we *act*?"

"Alexi." My wife tugged at my sleeve and reminded me of the time. The gas lamps in the streets would already be glowing yellowy-white in the gently falling snow. The trams would soon stop, and the night patrols would be out.

"What we need is action. Some say action isn't — can never be — democratic. But just look at what we are up against. The searches, the identity cards, the curfews."

Conversations stopped. Faces turned towards me, Peter's amongst them, a macabre interest in what was about to come. Like onlookers watching an accident unfold.

"But some people, the people who laughingly claim to be in opposition, implore us to *construct our resistance within the democratic framework*, or some other such nonsense. But they are just puppets, their strings worked by the Government to give the appearance of freedom. But it's all a charade, a chimera."

"What do you suggest, Professor Doubravou?" a voice called.

I recognized her vaguely, a former assistant in the politics department. A self-proclaimed specialist who had once penned a minor pamphlet on moral philosophy, or the concept of freedom, or some other angels-on-the-head-of-a-pin nonsense.

"I think the professor is referring to direct action," Peter declared. "Anarchism. Bringing down the Government by force. Paralyzing our leaders by forcing them to write out pi to the last decimal place possible." He smiled and raised his glass to me in mock tribute. A few others laughed politely, the tension broken.

That was the moment I could have confirmed it all as a joke, walked away from the mess I was creating. Instead, I slapped the arm of the chair, jarring my glass, slopping wine.

"Exactly. Anarchism. I have gauss sabots, live rounds for a magnetic coilgun, totally silent. But I don't have the gun. I kept some ammunition after the War. I wasn't meant to. But I did. But if only I had a gauss gun ..."

My grim-faced wife tugged at my sleeve. "Alexi. Maybe we had better get home."

"Professor, is it better to die for something you believe in, or to kill for it?" the young woman called out, as if asking whether I wanted my tea with or without lemon.

"Why, kill, surely," I said, managing to match her poker-face. For an aging lecturer of mathematics, my words were so outrageous they surely could not be mistaken for anything other than comedy.

"To die for a cause changes nothing, and what is a cause if it is not the desire to change the world? No, if the choice you give me is binary, then only by killing can you change the world. You might end up dying for your cause, but you must set out to kill. Anything else is just romanticism and empty gestures."

All eyes were on me, the aged drunken thinks-he's-a-firebrand. Jaws were ajar. Somebody coughed in embarrassment. My joke had misfired. I had misjudged the mood.

From the next room shrill conversation carried over. "… I said, *You promised to show me a good time*, and he said, *But I did. I showed you plenty of people having a good time*." Their raucous laughter broke the ice that had formed over my audience. As if in slow motion, people turned to their neighbor or searched for drinks or coats.

"Well, Alexi, you certainly shook them up," Peter said as they began to disperse. "Do you think they realize you were being satirical? Humor is not something we expect from the Department of Mathematics."

Sergei, I knew, could be relied on to choose his guests wisely, but two were utterly unknown to me. One was a young man in a borrowed suit, fat-jowled and sunken eyed before his time, forever eating. His reactions to my impromptu sermon had been equally stupefied.

The other, a young woman with alabaster skin and raven hair plastered back wearing a man's suit, severely waisted, as if she were on her way out for a morning canter. A pince nez added a spinsterish quality. She had been at the shoulder of the ex-assistant from the politics department whose bait I had taken all too greedily. Whilst it had been her companion who had goaded me, in her silence she had taken me seriously. Deadly seriously. And that troubled me.

Peter laughed at my concern. "The young man? That's Maria's brother, no … half-brother, I think. An idiot. Understood nothing, not one jot. Like a priest in a whorehouse."

"Please, Peter — is he liable to report me?"

"He is Maria's half-brother, that's good enough for me."

"And the other girl? She was with the one who worked in the politics department. White skin, black hair, pince nez. About so high ..."

"Girl? You mean woman ..."

"I am seventy-five, you are thirty-five. To me she was a girl." I rubbed my forehead. The hangover was starting before the party had even finished. "A word in the wrong ear ..."

My wife again tugged at my sleeve. "Alexi. I think we ought to go. The curfew ..."

"Yes, the curfew, Alexi. To be reported for treason is one thing," Peter guffawed, "to break the curfew is quite another."

•   •   •

In Sergei's absence — the party was to celebrate his going away for some months — I made discrete enquires as to the identity of the former politics assistant's companion, but nobody could tell me anything specific. A friend of a friend, an acquaintance of an acquaintance. A bookseller, a poet, a milliner. Each time she changed shape and name. At one moment Nadia, at another Katya, then Anna. In every case a different person was being referred to. It was as if she had never been at Sergei Popov's party.

"Perhaps she's Avakardian," Peter suggested in an icy whisper.

Avakardian. Malice personified; evil made flesh. But only if you believed in goblins and trolls. A new bogeyman for mothers to threaten errant children with. The footsteps in the snow behind you after curfew. A name that had come from nowhere, and now seemed to be the punchline to every macabre joke.

"Ridiculous. A pantomime villain. There is no Avakardian," I said.

As the days passed, the question of the agitator's — as I had come to think of her — companion slipped from my mind. Peter was right, Sergei would have chosen his guests wisely. I focused on my work: number pattern evolution theory. A grid is drawn up, with a first row of numbers assigned at random, one, two, or three, say. A set of rules then defines the numbers in the row below: 'If the number above is equal to the number above and to the right, but different to the number above and to the left, insert the number two', and so on. These rules generate a cascade of further numbers, on and on, potentially forever.

There was nothing new in this area of research. A British mathematician, Conway, had invented it as a frivolous game seventy years' before. With the science of computing burgeoning, it had attracted a following, a cult, even. But the Pulse put an end to the Data Age at a stroke, transforming anything reliant on laborious computation into an academic backwater. But, somehow, I was attracted to swimming in backwaters.

My self-appointed quest was to find why certain rules threw up repeating patterns, complex beyond beauty — by using colors for numbers a convincing imitation of the party symbol had even appeared — whereas others caused only banality or randomness. What did one set of algorithms have which was absent in the others? These were the questions that I let fill my mind, not the identity of a myopic stranger.

When the Party symbol emerged, I showed Peter, who was more intent on explaining a barmpot theory that the energy of the first Pulse, the Sun's aberration which destroyed the technology the world then relied on, may have split space and time. That a parallel existence had been created and may, perhaps, survived intact. *Would you not do anything to get there*, he wondered.

I dismissed these ravings and pulled him back to my pattern-making. Barely interested, he suggested allowing errors to creep in, to see whether patterns would reassert themselves like a jogged spinning top, or if they would collapse or even evolve anew. I was furious. Typical of a physicist to be so blasé over errors, but for a mathematician?!

But it was a stroke of genius.

I ended up taking almost sadistic pleasure in wrongfooting my two assistants, graduate students, changing outputs, seemingly on a whim. I would then return an hour or so later to see what damage I had produced.

When the knock came at my study door, I naturally assumed one of my assistants had come to show me the results of my meddling. But it was not. It was the former politics assistant. Dressed in an oversized shapeless coat, I did not recognize her at first.

"I am sorry. I startled you," she said, hovering at the threshold.

"Not at all." I waved her towards the chair opposite. I wanted to end this now, here.

"I was impressed by what you said at Doctor Popov's gathering. Few would have felt as free to express their opinions."

Could she be an informer for the Party? I had to work quickly if I were to limit any damage. "I was drunk," I barked. "Think nothing of what I said."

"Professor," the woman leant forward in astonishment. "I cannot think nothing of what you said. You were inspirational."

"I was drunk." I feared the direction the conversation was heading.

"Sometimes the drunken man can see the truth the sober man cannot."

"... and the most foolish man can ask questions which the wisest cannot answer."

I was mocking her, but my words had missed their mark.

"Yes, yes ... the most foolish man." Her eyes blazed for a second, in recognition of a kindred spirit, I'd venture. "You asked questions of all of us, but we are not foolish, you and I, Professor. We are wide-awake whilst so many others sleep in this city. We know what we must do. Direct action."

"I was playing devil's advocate."

She shook her head. "I saw it in your eyes, professor. I heard it in your voice."

And then she reached into her coat and brought out a bulbous object wrapped in brown cloth. She placed it on the table with a dull metallic thud and let the cloth fall away.

I stared at its alien form. It looked like some creature, shiny black, having just emerged from a river or swamp, coiled, about to spring. Or like an oversized molded fist in a leather glove, a smoothly bored forefinger extended, pointing. A Gauss gun, designed to magnetically accelerate and project a bullet.

"This still works, Professor. The photovoltaic cells covering it still charge. The Sun, the Sun that destroyed the old technologies, still powers this. It was designed to survive the electromagnetic discharge of a nuclear weapon so, of course, it survived the Pulse."

The young woman stared at me with the calm serenity of a believer in possession a holy relic. A relic I refused to have any dealings with as I made plain. If she was a Party informer here to tempt me, then I wanted her to remember my ire.

"If you won't use the tools of revolution, then there is something I want you to do for me, Professor. I have the gun, here in my hand. But I do not have any projectiles. You have Gauss sabots, but no gun. I want you to give me your rounds."

"My rounds? But how do you know they will fit? The caliber ..."

"They will fit, or they will be made to fit," she declared.

And then I began to laugh. The tension dissolved from my body. "But I have only four sabot rounds. Four rounds for a Gauss pistol is hardly enough for a revolution."

"Four rounds will be enough for what I intend," she said, without the slightest deflection to her zealotry.

I smiled, trying to ease us away from the brink. "I'm not your man. I am all bluster, nothing more. The piss and wind of an old man. Perhaps I could have helped, once. But not now. Please go on your way. Forget all this."

She paused at the door. "There is somebody I want you to meet," she said evenly. "She may change your mind."

·   ·   ·

They were waiting for me in one of the smaller lecture

halls, rising horseshoes of dark wooden counters with bench seats behind, the smooth arcs broken into thirds by two aisles that ascended to double doors at the rear. The arrangement focused in on a large desk front and center with multiple blackboards behind covered in Greek letters, algebra and equations.

The young woman formerly of the Department of Political Philosophy ran a finger back and forth on the mahogany of the lecturer's desk as though assessing the dusting. She looked irritated, but I put it down to nerves. The one I was there to meet, her companion from Sergei's party, sat at the end of the front row, pushing herself into the shadows. At the party, make-up had made her look young, the pince nez an old-before-her-time affectation. Now her face, grey and lined, had caught up with her eyewear.

"I wasn't sure you'd come," said the former politics assistant.

I almost hadn't. But I wanted to hear what they had to say and then draw a line under the whole matter, consign it to history.

"Ask me where I've been," the seated woman said with a tobacco hoarseness that added another five years to her. Suddenly they could be mother and daughter.

I shrugged and asked.

"A little village called Shavici."

It meant nothing to me.

"Ask me what's in Shavici."

My face registered irritation at the game — *just tell me what you want to tell me and have done with it —* but I asked anyway.

"The People's Correction Centre FG35."

My irritation turned to surprise tempered by suspicion.

The young woman smiled mockingly. "You didn't think anybody ever came *out* of a People's Correction Centre."

"I'm not even sure I believed they existed."

The older woman looked up at me. "Where do you think the disappeared go?"

"I assumed they just disappeared," I said. What I meant, of course, was 'taken outside and shot'.

"Not all," she said, reading my thoughts, and pulled down her shirt collar, revealing a string of numbers crudely tattooed blue-green. "Do you know what happens in the camps?"

"Breaking rocks? Sewing mailbags? How should I know?"

"We sit at desks for fifteen hours a day. Sacks of letters are brought to us. We have long lists of words, phrases — *bomb*, *assassination*, *plot* — and names, hundreds of names. We to go through the letters. Find them. Log them."

"Why do you think the mail takes ten days to go from one town to the next?" the former politics assistant broke in. "Because it gets diverted to a correction camp where every item is opened and gone through."

"I have seen your name, Professor," the older woman said.

"On one of your lists? A name to look out for?" I smiled skeptically. I couldn't see myself handing over the gauss sabots if this were the best they could come up with.

"No. But it occurred close enough to others to feature on the grey list."

"The grey list?"

"Candidates to be added to the main liSt Potential fellow travelers."

"I see." Although I wasn't sure I did.

The woman reached into a pocket and pulled out a black rectangular object I immediately mistook for a cigarette case. I was about to say she could not smoke in the theatre, but my words caught in my throat as the black rectangle ... lit up. Placing it on the desk, she softly growled my name, my full name, at the device and a cone of blue light burst upwards, like a bunch of flowers from the hand of a circus clown.

I drew near, incredulous.

Within the cone of light were moving images of me walking, lecturing, drinking coffee. I could see the most recent letter I had written to my cousin was uppermost on a concertina of virtual paperwork. With a practiced flick of her fingertips, she moved through them. I caught other letters I had written, departmental correspondence, examples of number pattern evolution. She tapped on a hovering dot and we heard me say — through an unseen, but crystal-clear speaker — some dismissive remark from a café, *not even good enough to polish my buttons*, that I did not even remember making.

With a finger-click the projection vanished, the device rapidly secreted.

"That isn't possible," I stammered. "Computers are no longer viable. The Pulsing of the Sun ... silicon circuitry is fried within moments. If computers were possible, we'd ..."

"Be a democracy?" the ex-politics assistant mocked.

"There is no solar pulsing," the ex-prisoner said. "A government myth."

Like Avakardian, I thought to myself. I felt weak in the knees. The politics assistant helped me into a seat. "Will you give us those sabots now?" she asked.

"We must do more than that." I banged a fist on the desk. "We need to raise an army."

The only thing I raised were smirks on the faces of the two women. Not quite scornful, but certainly enjoying my reaction to having the veil pulled back. Handing over some aging ammunition suddenly seemed such a petty, pitiful contribution.

"There must be more I can do?"

The pair exchanged conspiratorial smiles, then the older huskily announced there was something else I could contribute to the revolution. And that I may even enjoy it.

•   •   •

The next morning, I left four gauss gun rounds in a carboard box in the student pigeonholes of the Department of Theological Philosophy under the name 'Schmitt'. Those were my instructions, and I carried them out to the letter.

As for the 'other thing', the two women were quite right. It did give me a certain spring in my step, a frisson anticipating when opportunity may present itself. In truth, I treated it like some childish game, and with childish games came childish giddiness.

But that was hardly surprising given what I knew. The rules of reality had just been turned on their head. Everything I thought was, wasn't. The game now was to spot the microphones, the cameras. Were they buried in walls and ceilings? Or, perhaps, hiding in plain sight, a secondary purpose to a lightbulb or a doorhandle I had never considered.

Unfamiliar with such technology, I had no idea what was possible. Perhaps the unseasonal fly that bothered me in my office was some man-made drone, watching and listening. But what hurt the most was that the daily grind of manual calculation I put my assistants through could have been accomplished in a fraction of a second, at how advanced my research could have been by then.

Hence, amid a dull departmental meeting, I found myself saying, "To quote the Credo of Comrade January, we are dealing with a conspiracy of violence."

The dean's secretary, taking notes, looked at me doubtfully. I felt a little glow of pride, thinking I had waved a meek and unassuming fist at the regime.

"Who is this Comrade January? I've heard you mention him twice," Peter asked me afterwards. "No — three times. I'm sure I heard you say the same thing in the coffeehouse."

"Just somebody I've read about."

"*The Credo of Comrade January*. You asked for it to be minuted."

"That's up to the minute taker."

"What is this all about?"

"It's just a phrase, Peter, just a phrase," I bristled, regardless of the truth.

As my two visitors had explained, if what I had seen was the weight of information the State had collected on me, a mere name on the grey list, a fellow traveler at worst, just imagine what was collected on real subversives. And imagine what the machinery of state would do if it were fed a name, a phrase which appeared to connect hither and thither, even if it meant nothing. It would tie itself in knots looking for links that were never there. Like Avakardian, Comrade January existed nowhere except in the imagination.

Peter shook his head sadly. An old man losing the plot. "In any case, that's not what I wanted to talk to you about. Would you review some calculations?"

"Yours?"

"No, a colleague's, but he would rather remain anonymous. You recall the theory that the Pulse affected time and space. Well, he has extended the theory and calculated the energies required to travel between the two. Even to *rejoin* the two spheres."

I smirked. "Fanciful nonsense. There are no parallel worlds."

"The theory is intriguing. In fact, downright persuasive. The Pulse did strange things. It gave people powers. Telekinesis, extra sensory perception."

"The Pulse caused modifications to our genetic structure that, for a fortunate few, manifested themselves in strange ways, but for millions meant cancer and death and, in every other respect, put our civilization back two hundred years. A series of events that led to war, pestilence, and book-burning. All we are doing in this ivory tower is relearning knowledge that was lost." I snatched my glasses from my face and wiped them furiously. I felt anger rising in my chest at what was not being said.

"Alexi," Peter persisted, as though he couldn't see how upset he was making me, "the work applies abstract number theory in incredible ways. Just as any positive number has two square roots, the theory says

the Pulse's energy was sufficient to split everything —
and everyone — in two. It created doppelgangers."

I held a hand up for Peter to stop. This way madness
lay.

But he barreled on. "What if we existed in two
worlds? What if the people we loved existed in two
worlds? What if we only lost them in one?"

And then it struck me. He wasn't being insensitive,
he thought he was helping. It was a scar that never went
away, but with my wife, my rock, we made it through
each day, one at a time. But we never forgot.

"The thing about abstract theory is that it applies
less often than we would like."

"Alexi, take a swinging pendulum, slowing down,
eventually stopping. To know a pendulum's motion
over time, you use the square root of negative numbers.
Imaginary numbers, but with real world implications.
It's not such a fantastic leap."

I wanted to shake him. "My children are dead,
Peter. I've come to accept that. There is no 'other world'
in which they live."

"The trouble with you, Alexi, is that you are a
mathematician. Your world is delineated, finite. In the
sciences, we *do*, we are still discovering."

"If I haven't succumbed to spiritualism and religion by
now, then I'm hardly liable to fall for poppycock arithmetic."

"In that case, look at the numbers and tell me where
it goes wrong?" He held out a folder of papers to me.
"Comrade January would want you to."

I sighed and, with great reluctance, nodded.

●   ●   ●

Impossibly large flakes of snow knocked against my office window as they tumbled earthwards. I had finished going through the theory from Peter's mysterious colleague for a second time, scribbling marginal notes, wondering how to insert a reference to Comrade January into my critical analysis. The logic was alluring, but mathematics is full of sleights of hand, smoke and mirrors, and even world-weary professors can find themselves down rabbit-holes. Like a well-practiced card player, I knew I was being cheated — I just hadn't yet worked out how.

It was then one of my assistants rushed in without bothering to knock. "The justice minister has been shot. A contraband weapon, apparently. A gas gun. Completely silent."

"What?" I leapt up with a horrible realization of what must have happened, of how the Chinese whispers had started already. "How? Where?"

"He was outside the municipal palace, getting into his limousine when he was shot."

"Who?"

"Nobody knows, but there's a riot going on. Crowds are fighting the police. They've ripped up the flagstones in the square. Korchenoi knows somebody in the telegraph office."

"Did they arrest him? The man who fired the shot?" I had to check myself to say 'man' and hoped my assistant would recall that detail, should it eventually matter.

"I don't know."

I felt nauseous. My head swam. I was sweating. Guiltily, I prayed the assassin, whichever one it was, had been killed as soon as she had carried out her deed.

I hurried home, my boots crunching through the icy crust of new snow. I decided to eschew the tram, even if it was still running; I needed the feeling of movement, of progress, of going forward. I needed the cut of cold air in my lungs. I needed to occupy my mind, to avoid thinking. It was all too horrible.

They came for me as I neared my apartment. Two men, one thin, one fat, identically dressed in long black leather coats. My concentration was on keeping my footing in the rutted snow, so I did not see them until I almost walked into them.

They put me in the back of a car, a rare sight. As it rolled past my apartment, I glimpsed a movement at the window. I murmured my wife's name. The officer next to me on the rear bench seat glanced over and then, considering me not a threat, let me be.

When we got to the police barracks, I was swept without ceremony into an interrogation room, relieved of my coat, jacket, shoes, socks, and pocket watch, and left in shirtsleeves in the unheated room. Nobody told me what to expect.

Time dragged. There were no windows, no clock. Echoing footsteps and muffled voices could be heard outside. The door fitted flush to the wall with no inner handle. Apart from the chair on which I sat, the desk I sat in front of, and the two chairs behind, there was nothing. Walls, floor, and ceiling were painted an icy white, washed yellow from the bare bulb overhead. A faint whiff of partially cleansed vomit hung in the air.

I was drifting off to sleep when they arrived. The door banged open, and I came to with a start. There were two of them, ordinary looking, businesslike. Under their suit jackets one had a burgundy sweater, the other grey herringbone. It was as though I was meeting a new dean of my faculty, or my bank manager. That was what I found most macabre.

"Could I have my jacket back? It's cold."

"I'm afraid that will not be possible until you leave," Burgundy said.

"And that won't be until you've furnished us with some answers," Herringbone added.

The first man spoke again. "Professor, tell me about your work."

A thought exploded like phosphorus in my mind. Was this about my research, not the murder of the justice minister or the 'credo' of a fictitious Comrade January? Was my work deemed to be outside the best interests of the Party and the People? How?

"Professor?"

I fumbled for an answer, my stomach clenched tight as a ball, my body shivering.

"It is difficult to explain to a lay audience. I am trying to think of terms you would understand ... analogies ..."

I embarked on an explanation of my research in simple language, complicated when my request for paper and a pencil was denied. Burgundy listened attentively. Herringbone smoked and looked bored. "Avakardian would get there quicker," he hissed at his colleague.

I choked back a laugh. Like fishwives, they had invoked a bogeyman. They weren't even good actors.

"That won't be necessary," Burgundy said ambiguously. "Professor, explain this."

The door opened and a guard carried in a long roll of paper. I recognized it as my number grid, the one that had formed a fair approximation of the Party symbol repeated and repeated, like lurid wallpaper.

"Yes, it is surprising the patterns that get thrown up. The simplest algorithms are often the most powerful."

"You expect us to believe this is just mathematics? Not some satire on the State?"

"You will find, on the back of the sheet, the algorithm."

They just stared at me, silent.

"The formula that generates the symbols," I explained. "The rules."

This facile nonsense was what this was all about? Were laughable patterns on paper what they took so seriously? I suddenly pitied them. There was no prescient, omniscient State machine, merely gullible people searching for clues in the dark.

"You call this a satire on the State. Perhaps it is an indication that the State is not an invention, but a discovery. We have discovered utopia." I waved a hand in the air; how I could have done with a cigarette between my fingers. "I'm only a mathematician, of course, not a social scientist, but I can see that it is a legitimate line of research."

With the click of the guard's heels, the paper was rerolled and whisked away.

"Professor, tell me about the people you work with."

Herringbone rolled sullen eyes at his colleague's question.

I decided to play garrulous, telling everything about my two assistants, their merits, their faults, their habits, their acquaintances. They asked about my wider circle of colleagues, other professors, who I would drink with in the coffee shops, who I would dine with in the university refectory. I couldn't believe I was putting a noose around anyone's neck.

"Professor, a crime of treason was committed earlier today."

I feigned bafflement. "The shooting? Is this what this is all about? What have I to do with it?"

"Plenty," Herringbone spat. "Why don't you just give us their names? We have your name, just give us the names of the other in the ring."

"The ring?" I was thrown by this change of tack.

"The circle, the group, the set, the cell, whatever you people call yourself. I don't care. I just want their names."

Burgundy held up his hand for silence.

"Give him to Avakardian," Herringbone cursed under his breath.

"Enough," Burgundy barked.

"Avakardian."

If this broiling disagreement was scripted to unsettle, it was quite effective. "I thought Avakardian was just a name in a modern-day folktale," I stammered.

"Avakardian is an unintelligent barbarian," Burgundy said. "But very, very efficient."

"His methods are more direct, cruder than ours. Less verbal, more physical," his colleague added, eager to let slip details. "In fact, Avakardian often doesn't care whether you give him the answers or not. He enjoys his work."

"There is no circle, no ring. I know nothing. I am just a professor of mathematics."

"They seemed to think you were somebody important. They gave us your name."

"My name?"

"Yours and Jesus and a Comrade January," Herringbone snarled. "We're still looking for the last two."

I went icy cold and began to gabble. "Maybe he is somebody from the university. Somebody who held me in respect and thought he was somehow revering me by carrying this act out. Students can get obsessive." It was a desperate thesis. They saw it in my eyes.

Burgundy asked, "So, you have reason to believe you know them?"

"How do I know unless you tell me who he is?" I wailed.

They conferred. I heard them refer to the mortuary.

I was marched down a long slate colored corridor, the floor cold against my bare feet. I shuffled, cowed. We went down steps — I guessed we were deep underground by then — until my two interrogators stopped at a set of double doors.

The mortuary smelt of something simultaneously chemical and culinary. Like a steak dressed in bleach. In the middle stood three slabs. On two, covered by cotton shrouds, lay bodies. Like magicians, they swept the covers back in unison to reveal two faces.

I knew they were studying me for a reaction, and I could not hide my shocked surprise. It took a moment for me to recognize them. They both looked different in death, the former assistant from the politics department and the stranger I first saw at Sergei's party. Not peaceful. Not happy. Sightless eyes open wide, mouths agape. They had died screaming.

"Women? Two women?" I had prepared this shocked reaction in my own head, but the sight of them made me blurt it out quite naturally. "They were at a party of Doctor Popov's, several weeks ago. I don't know her," I said of the one with the prison tattoo peeking out from the shroud. "The other used to have a minor role at the university, but in the politics department, not mathematics. I never knew her name."

"But you knew her face?"

Not that face, I thought as I nodded my assent.

"Professor, give me their names," the second barked. "Give me the names of the people you plotted this with, else ..."

He pulled the sheet down, revealing the torso of the former inmate of the People's Correction Centre FG35, Shavici. She was naked, her body as tight as the riding suit I first saw her in, her breasts pert and symmetrical, her skin a uniform alabaster, her nipples and areola remarkably dark. The only blemishes on her were two arcs of burn marks, five in each semi-circle, mirror images of one another, between her shoulders, below her throat. Her sister's — for I could see now that was who they were to each other — body was the same.

"Are those ..." *Fingers* was what I couldn't bring myself to say.

I spun around, conscious there was another in the room. Fat-jowled and hollow-eyed, I recognized him immediately, even if he was no longer dressed for a soiree. Maria's half-brother. But I was not sure he recognized me: there was a glassiness to his expression, like that of the extremely drunk or excessively tired. Had they taken him in at the same time as me? Had their questioning confused him to the point of collapse?

Then Maria's half-brother, the half-wit, placed his hands together, fingertip to fingertip, as if in quiet contemplation, and a web of blue sparks flew between them. The air crackled with a strange metallic smell, and I knew with sudden stomach-freezing certainty where the ten burn marks above the dead women's breasts had come from.

Avakardian's eyes caught mine, and recognition dawned. Would he recall my words at Sergei Popov's party? Would it even matter? He cracked a chilling smile and placed his fingers together again. But, instead of sparks, all that came was a smoky cough, a single blue flash. Childlike confusion was writ across his face.

"He's never done four in a day," said Herringbone. "In fact, he's never done three."

Avakardian turned to his keepers. "Hungry," he gurgled.

"Let's feed him well," agreed Burgundy. "This one can be kept on ice. Who knows how much he'll tell us in the meantime?"

"The cells are full of rioters," mused Herringbone. "But there's space for him in Frunzensky." He slapped a hand on Avakardian's shoulder, then glanced at me. "This one can be the first business of tomorrow. After a hearty breakfast."

He meant Avakardian, not me.

•   •   •

One knock, and the office door opened.

"Chief."

Yahnotov's grim expression and urgent tone meant he didn't need to spell it out. *Chief, there's been another one.*

At her desk overlooking the Neva River, Katarina Preobrazhensky turned away from her screen. She had been working through autopsy evidence. She massaged her temple, warding off the first tremors of a migraine. It was too warm for this time of year. Again.

"This one's different," Yahnotov said, closing the office door behind him and handing her, firstly, a pair of black-lensed goggles in heavy plastic frames, followed by what looked like a mass of thimbles caught up in elastic bands.

Preobrazhensky slipped the goggles onto her face and her fingertips into the ten tiny receptacles. Yahnotov did likewise with a second set. After a moment of static she was there, looking down on another dead body with burns to his chest. This one was older than the last, and had been, at least, properly dressed — suit trousers and shirtsleeves — and properly fed.

"Same place?"

She scanned around. Evidently not the same place. An apartment block, three stories, landscaped with cabbage trees and yucca. Middle class housing. They were in the parking lot. A Mercedes sat at an angle, a man with a worried expression stood at an open driver's door.

"Frunzensky."

Preobrazhensky flinched, making her drone, five miles distant, wobble in the air. Quite an achievement, given the continual storms they already had to counterbalance.

"Frunzensky?" Katarina Preobrazhensky was Chief Inspector of the Main Criminal Investigations Directorate of the Main Administration for Internal Affairs of the City of St Petersburg and the Leningrad Oblast for Vasileostrovsky District. Not Frunzensky District, *Vasileostrovsky* District.

Preobrazhensky turned to Yahnotov, seeing just his accompanying drone, long tentacles hanging, ready to react to her colleagues' finger movements. "Why aren't Frunzensky handling this?"

"Because what's distinctive isn't where it is."

She grunted and went back to examining the body. She couldn't argue with that. If only the first six, or maybe just the first one, had turned up in Frunzensky District, then maybe she could just be a spectator to this investigative poisoned chalice.

"At least this one isn't covered in shit," she said.

"Nor snow."

Another grunt. Emptying your bowels because several thousand volts are being passed through you, she could understand. But snow? In St Petersburg? There hadn't been snow this far south in years.

"Patrol will be there in three minutes," Yahnotov said, and, as if on cue, faint sirens could be heard in the distance.

"So, we have six bodies, of people we cannot trace, who haven't been reported missing, in prison garb, *but not our prison garb*, tortured, starved, beaten, burns on their body centered on their chest and shoulders, all dumped in the same location despite surveillance being in place for the last two and now ... where exactly are we?"

"Ulitsa Samoylovoy. A small apartment parking lot near the Lutheran cemetery. He's lying in plain sight, on the sidewalk, across the entrance. A man was about to drive to work. Swears he wasn't there a moment ago. Swears he saw nobody dump a body."

"I believe him," she said. What was one more impossibility amongst all the other impossibilities they had so far logged?

Using the drone's tentacles, she pulled at the victim's shirt to examine the burn marks, two arcs of five, matching the other six cadavers. It had been a decent garment at one point, but it had been shredded by whatever had happened.

"He's barefoot," she commented.

"Says there was a barbeque smell when he got out of his car and saw the body, the body that wasn't there when he got in," Yahnotov continued.

Switching to infrared confirmed the corpse was still warm, suggesting it had only been recently deceased, but given it may have had enough energy put through it to make a slab of frozen meat glow, it was far from a cut-and-dried conclusion.

"Tell patrol to seal the area, fingertip search the vicinity, take statements, check camera feeds," she said hollowly.

If asked what for, the only answer she could offer would be a flippant 'clues'. She knew they would find nothing because there would be nothing to find. She knew the body — unchipped, she'd wager — would defy tracing, that DNA samples, retinal scans, and dental records would prove wild goose chases, as if the corpse had dropped from outer space or risen from the ground. She knew there would be no witnesses worth interviewing. But she had to go through the motions.

One lead was all she wanted. One moment of hope, one way into this enigma.

Katarina Preobrazhensky's police drone hovered above the body. She could hear the sirens closer now. Yahnotov muttered instructions to the patrol officers about to arrive. She drummed her fingers on her desk. There was no such thing as an unsolvable case, no genuine locked-room mystery. There was always a flaw in the logic, a chink in the armor.

"It's the Pulse," Yahnotov said balefully, a figure of speech for anything unfortunate or unplanned or inexplicable, citing the bump in the road of history four decades earlier from which the world had swiftly recovered. His children were now taught it in history class. They preferred wars.

One lead. Was that so much to ask?

And then she saw it. A flutter of an eyelid. The merest twitch around the mouth.

"He's alive." It came out as a croak, the words stuck in her throat. "Get an ambulance," she yelled. "Tell patrol. He's alive."

•　　•　　•

I took some time to adjust to the gloom, everything so shades of grey I did not initially realize I was awake, that I was staring at off-white ceiling tiles, inset lights turned down to a milky glow. I tilted my head. I was in a hospital bed, floor to ceiling glazing separating me from the ward proper. Tubes and wires ran from my nose and midriff to fantastical machines which beeped and throbbed. Everything looked sleek and clean and molded, like the devices of our youth which now languished in museums of the Data Age.

"How are you feeling?"

I eased myself up on an elbow, rolled my head so far, my eyes a little further. There were four people in the room with me. The doctor was a middle-aged Mongol, concern etched across his face. Behind him half a pace, a woman with long blonde hair and a younger colleague, both businesslike and stern. And, behind them, just out of sight ... The man stepped forward, making it easier for me to see.

The woman introduced herself brusquely as Katarina Preobrazhensky, Chief Inspector of something with an impossibly long name for City of St Petersburg and the Leningrad Oblast, for Vasileostrovsky District. She asked me whether I knew the man.

I shook my head, but could not help but whisper, "It's me."

The Chief Inspector exchanged glances with her colleague. It was the answer they expected but least wanted.

I looked at all the things that did not make sense. The machines. Lights seamlessly set into the ceiling. Police that introduced themselves by name.

"I cannot feel my legs," I said. "I was cold. Now I cannot feel anything." Panic rose. Perhaps frostbite. Perhaps they had been amputated.

"We've administered painkillers," the doctor soothed. "You've suffered burns. But you have all your limbs, all your extremities — toes, fingers — all there."

Preobrazhensky cut in. "Doctor, explain this. DNA, fingerprints, dental scans, all match. Even childhood scarring. In a court, this man," she glanced at me, "could prove he was that man. How is this possible?"

The doctor's body language was clear. This was beyond him. "You have two minutes. Nothing taxing," he ordered. "Then he must rest."

I sensed my doppelganger had been permitted to stay and listen. The two police officers barraged questions, purely factual. My biography, my history, my family. Where I was when the Pulse happened, what I did in the years after. I closed my aching eyes and answered them briefly and plainly. I heard a mutter from the corner when our stories diverged, an intake of breath when my children died.

Then a door clicked, and I sensed the acoustics change and heard the doctor's voice curtailing my interrogation. A rustle as people stood, moved, and then my doppelganger asked about Helena.

"I don't think I'll ever see her again," I whispered.

"She's alive? In your world, she's alive?" Disbelief, joy, wonder.

"Doctor Doubravou, please," the physician said, shepherding the room empty.

A moment later I felt a tear slide down my cheek. For him, Doctor Alexi Doubravou, Helena lost; for me, Professor Alexi Doubravou, Sasha and Kolya.

●　　　●　　　●

There followed a succession of assessments and interrogations. I was evaluated physically. I was evaluated psychiatrically. I was evaluated academically. I knew they wanted to conclude that I had constructed a delusional alternative reality, richly detailed, internally consistent. But what prevented them from institutionalizing me was, of course, my doppelganger. Less a fly, more an imperial eagle in the ointment, the co-existence of me and the impeachable Doctor Doubravou, not to mention the previous six corpses Avakardian had sent between worlds plus another five since my arrival, meant that nothing outside Aristotle's three laws of thought was now deemed impossible.

Chief Inspector Preobrazhensky's visits grew less frequent and less urgent; what could she do with what I had told her? Contact with Doctor Doubravou was not encouraged. He found my existence troubling. I could hardly blame him; I found existence itself troubling. I asked to see his — my? — children, but the psychologists deemed it unwise. In any case, they were grown and lived far away from St Petersburg and were equally confused and perturbed. I suspected only my doppelganger could truly empathize. He had just learnt his Helena lived on, somewhere unreachable. His pain was my pain. But a pain he did not wish to share.

I was put in a convalescent room on an upper floor from where I could watch the roiling clouds gather and attack at speed from the Gulf of Finland over Kotlin Island, as if the city itself was galloping into the weather. They never stopped. My St Petersburg was bright white, glistening and soft-edged, like an iced cake. This city was grey and sharp-cornered, all slab-sided concrete and harsh electric illumination. There were no lamplighters here. I watched the sequencing of traffic lights, the blue crackle of trains, faces pressed at the carriage windows far below. Where were so many people going? What did they do? Snow used to pirouette from the sky. Now lightning forked and rain lashed, easing briefly before another wave bowled in.

My room was more akin to a hotel than a hospital room. Unfamiliar clothes hung on wire coat-hangers and I was encouraged to dress and use the communal areas when I felt strong enough. When I did not, I could lie in bed with everything within easy reach and, if power were needed for my entertainment or care, a rail ran around the room at chest height into which a sleek plug could be inserted at any point. Ingenious.

My stamina was not what it was. My heart had been damaged. But I did not want to stand in the way of their understanding the St Petersburg that lay so close but so far away. I answered every question as well as I could, whether about me or the city, without evasion, except for one thing. I never told them about Peter's theory of parallel worlds and its implications for joining the two together.

Yes, I realized it was Peter's theory. He was no front for some anonymous researcher. It was his work. After giving me his papers to review he had described me as being like a square root: just as people only think of one of two possible answers, I was only ever seen as a tired, skeptical, cynical mathematics professor. But Peter thought there was another side to me that could seize the moment, answer the call to arms. In my speechifying at Sergei's he glimpsed that other facet. My broadcasting the name Comrade January would have proved it for him, had he known its meaning. His theory, his brilliant theory: that was his other square root, the one everybody forgot to remember.

I broke the coat hanger, straightened out the wire, made sure the tip was sharp. It was time to act. It was time for me to be that forgotten root.

I asked to see Doctor Doubravou. One last time. There were matters I wished to discuss, I said. In private. If I could be granted this one wish.

He came.

I was in bed. I only moved my eyes when he entered, smiled weakly. He drew the only plausible conclusion, that I was dying, that the doctors had downplayed my condition.

He drew up a chair and I made sure he heard my labored, erratic breathing. I whispered one word — "Helena" — and beckoned him closer.

He leant over me. I placed my hand over his. He leaned closer to my mouth to catch my words. Unnoticed, I felt for the straightened coat-hanger wire under the sheets.

I brought my free hand up and out as I had rehearsed and swung it hard and true, plunging the coat-hangar wire into the powerrail where it ran above my headboard.

There was a sparking, a burning. I felt a mule's kick and a shaking to my core. My hands involuntarily gripped both the wire and my doppelganger. Doctor Doubravou's face convulsed in a rictus grin, his eyes bulged wide. The ceiling lights flickered. But that was not why the world turned black.

What happens when you add the two roots of any number? They cancel each other out. They sum to zero. That was what Peter's theory had said. The two Doubravous: him, the doctor; me, the professor. We cancelled each other out. Like light and dark, heat and cold, matter and anti-matter.

But Peter had only seen so far. He could have driven his theory into stranger territory. He was, after all, a physicist, constrained by the real world. In the hands of a mathematician, numbers can be cajoled to perform extraordinary magic. He never thought to ask what zero can achieve. He simply thought the answer was nothing.

You see, zero has no weight, no effect, no impact. Which means it can be nowhere — or anywhere, everywhere, all at once, without unbalancing anything one iota.

I — the two Doubravous, Doctor and Professor — had become zero. We were nothing. Between this world and the other, in both and neither. A metaphysical miasma. Everywhere and anywhere. In space and time.

Only I had seen this in Peter's theory. Only I had pursued the numbers to the vantage point of the gods, with every event in the two worlds that had ever happened within sight.

And, oh, what sights.

I was with the justice minister as he was shot. I was with Helena as she fretted at home for me. I was a young man watching the sun pulsate. I was with my children, alive and adult and showing me their own children.

I was in the future, watching Chief Inspector Katarina Preobrazhensky climb the palace's marble steps backed by soldiers from her own world, her blonde tresses billowing in the snow flurries. I was there as Avakardian lunged at her, his fingertips sparking, to which she responded by putting three swift rounds into him.

Did I say she?

I meant to say *we*. For I am zero. I am your conscience and your judgment. I am your indecision and your impulsive recklessness. I am your gnawing doubt and the new ideas that spring afresh in your mind.

I pulled Katarina Preobrazhensky's finger on that trigger.

I killed Avakardian.

For a brief moment every action, every event, every thought, every idea, every person who had ever lived and breathed, ran through me, through us, the two Alexis.

My doppelganger's weight shifted, breaking the circuit, splitting us back into our constituent parts. But a hole between realities remained, and Doctor Doubravou was at risk of falling through. I could see my St Petersburg, snowy St Petersburg beneath him. Two people in fur hats pointed up at what, to them, must have been an inexplicable rip of light in the sky, two men looking down, one dangling through the rent, his legs kicking.

Snow. I felt snow on my face.

Ashen faced, Doctor Doubravou hauled himself up onto the bed, shaking, moaning. He was, after all, seventy-five years old, had just been electrocuted, spread across time and space, and then found himself dangling two hundred and fifty feet above the ground of an alternative reality. He had every right to jibber.

Alarms screamed in my room from the corridors outside.

The bed teetered on the junction of two worlds, the edge of a hole from one reality to another. And the rent was growing, like tissue paper in a storm, shredding, tearing, vanishing. I had run the numbers in my head, but could not be sure whether, like my patterns, the rip would run away uncontrollably or find a new stability.

Footsteps pounded in the corridor outside. The door to my room was yanked open and a doctor stared incredulously in, blanching at the cold, her hair caught in the breeze, looking through a hole towards the Gulf of Finland.

Voices echoed in my head. There was a strange taste in my mouth. I knew what was happening — the numbers had predicted this too. Whilst it had taken all Avakardian's energy to push me from one reality to the other, for the joining of doppelganger pairs I knew a small current would suffice. In theory, not even a lethal current.

Perhaps not lethal for him ...

From the tightness in my chest I knew I was not long for this world. The greying of my vision was more than just freezing fog created by mild moist hospital air meeting arctic temperatures. I laughed as snow hit my face, huge soft white flakes of the stuff. I may not live to be there, but I had seen the future. It went beyond Chief Inspector Katarina Preobrazhensky killing Avakardian. My doppelganger and his children would find my Helena and be a family again. Peter would take the credit for explaining the inexplicable. This St Petersburg would overwhelm the despotism of mine. But it had been me that had started the revolution. Comrade January would be proud.

As I took my last breath, I knew my St Petersburg would have peace again — and this other St Petersburg, snow.

ABOUT THE AUTHOR

Robert Bagnall was born in Bedford, England. He has written for the BBC, national newspapers, and government ministers. Four of his stories have been selected for the annual *Best of British Science Fiction* anthologies. His science fiction thriller *2084 - The Meschera Bandwidth*, and anthology *24 0s & a 2*, which collects 24 of his seventy-plus published stories, are both available. He can be contacted via his blog at *meschera.blogspot.com*.

YOU MIGHT ALSO ENJOY

REDUCTION IN FORCE
by Steve Soult

A heartless corporate layoff leaves Gil Schaffer emotionally shattered. A revolutionary memory erasure procedure may be his only hope for salvation, but the price could be greater than he bargained for.

SAYING GOODBYE
by J Dark

A young girl, searching for the parents who abandoned her, discovers that some answers only lead to more questions.

SEVEN OF SWORDS
FROM "THE STORYTELLER'S TAROT"
by L. A. Jacob

Thievery, trickery, something precious is stolen.

Available in digital and trade paperback editions from
Water Dragon Publishing
waterdragonpublishing.com